The Little Wooden Shoe

by

W.C. Van de Hulst

illustrated by
Willem G. Van de Hulst, Jr.

INHERITANCE PUBLICATIONS
NEERLANDIA, ALBERTA, CANADA
PELLA, IOWA, U.S.A.

Library and Archives Canada Cataloguing in Publication
Hulst, W. G. van de (Willem Gerrit), 1879-1963
[Klompje dat op het water dreef. English]
    The little wooden shoe / by W.G. Van de Hulst ; illustrated
by Willem G. Van de Hulst, Jr. ; [translated by Harry der Nederlanden].
(Stories children love ; 1)
Translation of: Klompje dat op het water dreef.
Originally published: St. Catharines, Ontario : Paideia Press, 1978.
ISBN 978-1-928136-01-9 (pbk.)
    I. Hulst, Willem G. van de (Willem Gerrit), 1917-, illustrator
II. Nederlanden, Harry der, translator III. Title. IV. Title: Klompje dat
op het water dreef. English V. Series: Hulst, W. G. van de (Willem Gerrit),
1879-1963 Stories children love ; 1
PZ7.H873985Lit 2014   j839.313'62   C2014-903591-8

Library of Congress Cataloging-in-Publication Data
Hulst, W. G. van de (Willem Gerrit), 1879-1963.
[Klompje dat op het water dreef. English]
    The little wooden shoe / by W.G. Van de Hulst ; illustrated by Willem G. Van de Hulst, Jr. ;
edited by Paulina Janssen.
    pages cm. — (Stories children love ; #1)
    "Originally published in Dutch as Het klompje dat op het water dreef. Original transla-
tions done by Harry der Nederlanden and Theodore Plantinga for Paideia Press,
St. Catharines-Ontario-Canada."
    Summary: After a miller finds a little wooden shoe floating on the water, his entire town
becomes concerned that a child has come to harm except one little boy with a guilty
secret, but when he is found out, he is in for a big surprise.
    ISBN 978-1-928136-01-9
    [1. Lost and found possessions—Fiction. 2. Behavior—Fiction. 3. Community life—
Fiction. 4. Secrets—Fiction.] I. Hulst, Willem G. van de (Willem Gerrit), 1917-
illustrator. II. Title.
PZ7.H887Lit 2014   [E]—dc23   2014017981

Originally published in Dutch as *Het klompje dat op het water dreef*
Cover painting and illustrations by Willem G. Van de Hulst, Jr.
Original translations done by Harry der Nederlanden and Theodore Plantinga
for Paideia Press, St. Catharines-Ontario-Canada.
The publisher expresses his appreciation to John Hultink of Paideia Press for
his generous permission to use his translation (ISBN 0-88815-501-8).

Edited by Paulina Janssen

ISBN 978-1-928136-01-9

Published simultaneously in U.S.A. by Inheritance Publications
Box 366, Pella, Iowa 50219

Printed in Canada

Contents

1. Small and White

The miller was an old man.
He was standing by the water.
And the red sun was about to go to sleep, far away
between the golden clouds.

But, look! Over there . . . On the water!
Look! What was that drifting on the water?
It was small and white.
The old miller peered. He scratched his head under
his cap. He always did that.
What was that on the water? What could it be? Small
and white? It came closer and closer.
Ah! Then he saw it, yes, then he saw it. It was
a wooden shoe, a little white wooden shoe.
It scared the old miller.

A wooden shoe on the water?

A small wooden shoe belonged to a little foot — yes, and that foot belonged to a little child.

But where was that child?

He did not see a child anywhere.

He looked across the water and along the road. He looked along the fields. No one.

It was very quiet everywhere. Night was falling. The golden clouds covered the red sun completely. It was getting dark. The little wooden shoe on the water drifted on like a little white boat on a dark sea. Soon it would drift right by.

But the old miller did not want that to happen.

He fetched a long stick and reached it out over the water.

He stabbed at the wooden shoe. Missed. Splash! Stabbed again. He had it!

The little white wooden shoe flew through the air and landed in the grass. The miller picked it up and looked at it. He scratched his head again. It sure was a little thing! It had to belong to a very little foot, a very little child.

But where could that little child be? Did it belong to a little boy? Or to a little girl?

The wooden shoe's mouth was wide open, but it said nothing.

Oh, that child . . .
Worried, the miller
looked out across the
water.
The water was so
dark. The water was
so deep.

2. A Serious Matter

Quickly, the miller walked away; he
almost ran. Down the dike he hurried,
carrying the wooden shoe. Again and again
he looked at the dark water. The miller's
wife saw him go, but she had not seen him find the
wooden shoe floating on the water. She was old; she
was sick. She spent her time sitting at the window
looking out over the fields.
"Where's that man off to now?" she wondered. "Why
is he in such a hurry at this time of night? I wonder
what's the matter."

The old miller walked on quickly.
Along the dike stood a house.
Children lived in that house, big ones and little ones.

It was quiet in the house. The shutters were closed.
The miller knocked on the door.
The mother answered, peering around the edge of
the door.
The miller asked, "Where are your children?"
"My children? In bed, of course."
"All of them?"
"Yes, all of them. I tucked them in myself — all six
of them. Why do you ask?"
"I found a wooden shoe. See? It was floating on the
water."
"On the water?" said the mother. "That's a serious
matter. And you don't know who it belongs to?"
"No," said the miller. "Not at all."
And he hurried off again.
The mother stepped back inside.
She quickly counted the little wooden shoes standing
by the door. Four — seven — ten — twelve! They
were all there! How happy she was!
Then the mother went to count her children. They
were all there too — all six of them. That made her
even happier. The children did not know that their

8

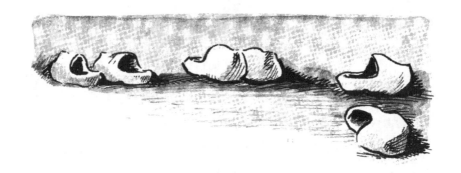

mother was counting them. They were asleep and dreaming.

Next the miller came to a big, beautiful home. In it lived a rich lady and a fat maid. But the lady never wore wooden shoes. And the fat maid had big wooden shoes that she wore when she scrubbed the steps of the big house.

No, the little wooden shoe had not come from that house.

The miller scratched his head and hurried on.

Next he came to a shoemaker's house.

Clop-clop! Clop-clop! went a hammer. The light from the lamp above the shoemaker's table shone through the window.

The shoemaker had a daughter. But, no, of course not!

Shoemaker's children don't wear wooden shoes.

So the old miller went on.

Next he came to a farmer's house.

The farmer had three sons, strong boys. But there were no little wooden shoes at that farm.

In the grass along the road sat a tramp. He was tired.
"Hi there," said the tramp.
"Good evening," said the miller. "Have you seen a little child around here? A little girl? A little boy?"
"Oh, sure. Hundreds of them," said the tramp. "Over there in the village. But they've all been called in and put to bed. One little girl brought me a sandwich. Looks good, doesn't it? There was a little boy sitting on the steps of the church. He was crying."
"Why?"
"I don't know."
"Was he wearing two wooden shoes?"
"I don't remember. I'm tired. A farmer is letting me sleep in his haystack tonight. Good night."
"Good night," said the miller. He forgot about the tramp. He looked at the little wooden shoe. He looked down the road toward the village. He looked at the dark water. Then he pushed back his cap and scratched his head.
The poor child! Where could it be? Was it a boy? Was it a girl?

He trudged on. A big frown was on his forehead. His eyes looked worried.
The quiet water flowed by slowly, as usual. The water was so dark; the water was so deep.

3. Foolish Little Rascals

Ah! A policeman was coming. Policemen usually knew what was going on. Oh! He turned down a side road.

"Hold it, Officer!" shouted the old miller. He waved the little wooden shoe in the air. "Wait a minute, Officer!"

The policeman jumped off his bicycle and waited. The miller hurried over and said, "Look at this. I fished it out of the water. But I do not know whose it is."

"Well, well," muttered the policeman. "Well, well. That doesn't look so good. It was floating on the water? What if the child wearing the wooden shoe . . ."

"Right, right!" nodded the miller. "If the child fell into the water too . . . And if only the wooden shoe drifted off . . ."

"Well, well," muttered the policeman again. "Well, well. Those foolish little rascals! Why would they play by the water anyway? It doesn't look good. But why don't you go back home now. I'll look after it. I'll ask around in the village."

The policeman jumped back on his bicycle.

The miller trudged back toward his windmill.

He took the wooden shoe with him.

Again and again he looked at the still dark water but the water told him nothing. It just flowed along slowly.

The moon shone that night.

The dark windmill stood still, dreaming. Its arms hung, like a big black cross in the silver light of the moon.

The windmill's owner, the old miller, lay in bed. He was dreaming too. He saw many, many children playing right by the edge of the water. Looking down from a window high in the mill he shook his fist at them and called, "You foolish little rascals! What are you doing playing by the water? It's deep there and very dangerous. Get away from there! Get away, right now! Watch out! Here I come!"

But the playing children just laughed at him. And then . . . then they all tumbled into the water, every one of them!

A splash, a ripple, and the water was still again.

Nothing but a row of wooden shoes floated on the water — little white wooden shoes.
Slowly they drifted away. The old miller gasped with fright.

His wife, lying next to him in bed, was not dreaming. She could not sleep. She lay there quietly looking around the small room as the silver light of the moon shone through the window.
She poked the old miller. "What's the matter with you? Are you dreaming?"
The old miller awoke, grumbled a bit, and rolled over. Then he fell asleep again.
But the old woman could not sleep. She lay there, her eyes wide open. On the mantel stood the little white wooden shoe. It was completely dry now. In the moonlight it shone like silver.
That poor wooden shoe! It had its mouth wide open, but it said nothing.
What foot did it come from?
What child did it belong to?
That poor child!
The water was so dark. The water was so deep!

4. The Wooden Crib

That night the moon also shone into a stable. In the stable a beautiful black horse stood fast asleep. Down its glossy back ran a shiny silver ribbon. That was the moon's doing.

The beautiful horse belonged to the mayor. Its name was Kuno.

And during the night a little mouse slipped into the manger.

It went straight for the feeding trough filled with the horse's oats. It nibbled and nibbled until its little mouse belly was round with delicious oats.

Oh, but then Kuno woke up.

He rattled the planks of his stall with his strong black legs. The horse scared the little mouse. Quick as a wink, he darted to a dark corner of the manger. Kuno was hungry for some oats himself. He pushed his big muzzle down into the oats and took a big bite. Bah! What was that? He bit into something hard, something that didn't taste good at all. It was small and white and round and wooden.

Roughly he shoved it aside. It rolled into the dark corner where the little mouse was hiding.

When Kuno had finished eating he went back to sleep. Then it was quiet in the stable once more. And then, yes, then the mouse dared to come out again. He did not want to eat any more. His little belly was as round and full as could be. All he wanted was a nice place to sleep. Quietly he crept into the wooden thing that had rolled into the corner of the manger. What a nice spot!

It was white and curved and hard. And it even had a roof! The little mouse hopped over the edge. He curled up deep inside. How nice! It was a beautiful wooden crib with a roof. Good night!

His little white crib was really a wooden shoe but the little mouse did not know that.

It belonged on someone's foot, on the foot of a little child, but he did not know that either.

And yes, it was the twin of the wooden shoe standing on a mantel in the windmill. The mouse did not know that at all. Who would have guessed it?

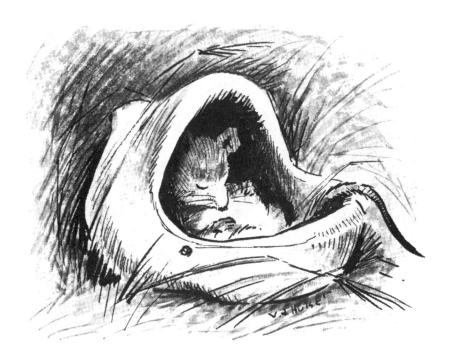

5. Identical Twins

It became morning.

The whole village woke up — then all the children

went back outside to play and all the fathers and mothers began to work. And then . . . the policeman began to look again and ask around. He went everywhere.

But no one knew anything about the wooden shoe that had floated on the water.

"Well, well," the policeman muttered. "Strange. I don't understand it. Maybe Sinterklaas left it behind."

All the mothers counted their children. The teachers at school counted the children too. Good! No one was missing.

How strange!

It became afternoon.

The old miller set the arms of his windmill turning merrily in the sky. His wife sat by the window again looking out over the fields. The wooden shoe stood on the mantel all alone.

And then . . . the policeman walked in.

"Well, well," he said. "Well, well. Look what I have here."

He put a little white wooden shoe on the table. Now there were two of them. And they were exactly the same size.

"Well, well! Look at that!"

The old woman stared with wide eyes.

"Another one? Another wooden shoe?"

The old miller stared too. He scratched his head even harder than usual.

"Another wooden shoe? One with a long thin string tied to it?"

The little wooden shoe's mouth was wide open but it said nothing. It was just as big, just as round, and just as white as the one on the mantel.

All three of them stared at the wooden shoes. They all shook their heads.

"Strange," said the policeman. "Strange."

The old woman asked, "Was this wooden shoe floating on the water too? My, my! Two wooden shoes from two little feet? Poor child!"

"No, no," said the policeman. "Not at all. It hasn't been in the water at all. It's as dry as can be. Just feel it. It was found in the mayor's stable in the manger with the oats. The mayor found it when he went riding on Kuno. He gave it to me."

"But how can that be?" muttered the old miller.

He scratched his

head again. How could the one wooden shoe end up floating on the water at night while the other wooden shoe ended up in the mayor's stable? They belonged together.

They were twins.

He put the wooden shoe with the other one on the mantel.

The long string hung down between them.

"How can that be? And no one knows whose they are. We've never had wooden shoes standing on our mantel before. And now suddenly there are two!" The old miller scratched his head with both hands at the same time.

"It sure is strange," the policeman said.

"My, my!" said the old woman. "My, my! And they're such pretty wooden shoes. They must belong to some nice little child."

And the wooden shoes?

They stood neatly beside each other on the mantel, the one just as round and just as white as the other. Both had their mouths wide open. But they said nothing.

6. Little Henry

A young boy sat at his desk in school.

His name was Henry.

The teacher said, "Henry, you are not looking in your book. You are daydreaming, Henry. Pay attention or you will have to stay after school."

Henry's face turned red.

Quickly he put his finger at the place where the class was reading.

Earlier that morning Henry had turned red too. The teacher had counted the students that morning. She had said, "Good. You're all here. Perhaps you heard that a small wooden shoe was found floating on the water by the windmill. That wooden shoe may belong to some boy or girl who was playing by the water and fell in . . . Oh, that would be terrible! But no one is missing a child. And no one knows whose wooden shoe it is."

No one?

Henry's cheeks burned. He ducked down so no one would see him. Would the teacher have seen him blush after all?

That horrible wooden shoe!

He couldn't get that wooden shoe out of his mind. And then he kept losing track of where the class was reading. And then he got scolded. All because of that dreadful wooden shoe!

Yes, but . . .

Yes, but it was really his own fault.

If only he had not done it!

What if the teacher found out?

What if his father found out?

What if his mother found out?

What if little Lydia found out?

What if that policeman who sometimes looked so grouchy found out?

The policeman was looking everywhere.
Henry had seen him that
morning. He had heard
the policeman mutter, "It
sure is strange."
That had been enough to
make Henry blush again.
He had quickly run away.
Yes, and now?
What would happen now?

What would happen when Mother came back?
And little Lydia? Oh, if Mother would start looking
— what then? If Mother heard about the wooden shoe
floating on the water by the windmill? Oh, what then?
What then?
Henry again lost the place where the class was
reading. His finger was lost on the page. It pointed
at the wrong word.

The teacher saw him.

She got even angrier than before.

She said, "Henry, you are dreaming again. You will have to stay after school."

At last it was four o'clock. The children were happy to go home. But Henry had to stay in school. There he sat, all alone in the room. The quiet, lonely room scared Henry.

That dreadful wooden shoe! That's why he had to stay after school.

Yes, but . . .

Yes, but it was really his own fault. If only he had not done it!

Big tears gathered in Henry's eyes.

7. If Only . . .

A little boy knelt by his bed. His hands were folded and his eyes were shut. Tears rolled down his cheeks. He felt so alone! And his heart hid a great fear.

Father was downstairs sitting in front of the house smoking his pipe and talking to the neighbor. Mother and Lydia were still away. Father had said, "Just think, Henry! Tomorrow Mother will be home again. And Lydia too. I'm glad of that. I'm sure you are glad too." He had also said, "A big boy like you can put himself to bed."

Now the little boy was kneeling by his bed, ready to pray — all by himself. But the little boy hid a great fear in his heart.

Mother had taken Lydia along to visit Grandma. They had gone by bus. But Henry had not gone along because he had to go to school. He was a big boy. And tomorrow Mother would be coming home again.

Oh, but those wooden shoes!

And it was all his own fault!

If only he had not done it!

The wooden shoes were gone — both of them! The wooden shoes belonged to Lydia.

Where were they now?

Yes, he had heard what the boys were saying on the street and what the mothers were talking about to each other. A wooden shoe had been found floating on the water all by itself, a little ways from the village. The miller had fished it out of the water and he had kept it.

That was one wooden shoe.

But what about the other one?

The other one was probably still in the mayor's stable or somewhere near it. The little boy did not know exactly where.

And now he had to pray.

He bowed his head right down to his hands. He prayed his usual evening prayer. Then he also whispered, "Dear Lord, it's my fault about the wooden shoes. I . . . I'm going to tell them everything."

Through the open window he heard his father and the neighbor talk and laugh.

If only the neighbor would go away!

If only Father was alone!

Then he would call through the window, "Father, Father, I have to talk to you."

Then Father would come. He would ask, "What's the matter, Henry?"

And then . . . then Henry would tell him everything. That would be very hard. Henry was afraid. Those two beautiful wooden shoes were missing! And he had done it.

Father would be very angry! And Mother too. And Lydia.

Maybe he should not tell after all. No one would know what he had done. No one had seen him.

No one . . . ? God in heaven had seen him! He saw everything. He knew everything.

Yes, Henry would have to tell.

He had promised in his prayer.

If only the neighbor would go away!

But the neighbor laughed and kept on talking. And Father laughed too.

Quietly Henry went to the window and looked out. It was dark outside. He crept back into bed. He would stay awake and wait until the neighbor would go away . . .

He closed his eyes. Just for a second. He would keep waiting.

Oh, but then Henry fell asleep anyway.

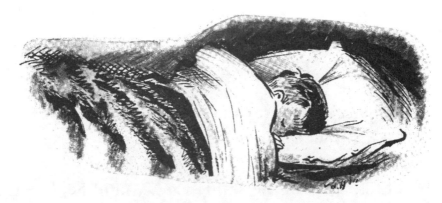

8. The Grumpy Mayor

And the next morning?
When Henry came downstairs, Father had already left for work.
A sandwich and a glass of milk stood ready on the table for Henry.
It was too late for Henry to tell his father now.

Look, Henry walked outside. But where was he off to? It was still so early in the morning. And he walked so carefully. Why?
He snuck into the mayor's yard. First he looked around carefully, his eyes full of fear.
At the back of the mayor's yard was the stable.
But — Henry knew he was not allowed to enter the mayor's yard. And certainly not the mayor's stable. If the mayor would see him . . . !
But he sneaked in anyway. Very fearfully. Very carefully. Very quietly. His heart beat wildly but he walked on. He walked on tiptoes, taking long careful steps.
He was close to the stable now.
He searched . . .
He searched in the grass; he searched in the bushes.
Oh, the wooden shoe was nowhere to be seen. Nowhere!
Should he look in the stable too? Would he dare?

The door was open
just a crack. Yes, he would!
He pushed the door open a little further . . . And
then a little further . . .

Oh, terrible!
Over there . . . ! Over there, next to the horse . . . !
There stood . . . !
Henry's heart jumped with fright. His knees almost
buckled.
There stood the mayor himself! He wore his riding
clothes and his riding whip was in his hand. He was
going to take Kuno for an early morning ride.
He heard the door squeak. The mayor turned around.

He saw the boy and called, "Who . . . what are you doing here?"

The frightened little boy stammered, "I . . . I . . . I . . ."

He tried again, "I . . . I . . . I . . ."

"I . . . I what? Speak up! What are you doing in this stable?"

"I . . . I am looking for the wooden shoe. Lydia's wooden shoe."

"The wooden shoe? You little rascal! Then you've been in this stable before."

"Yes . . . no . . . I . . ."

"What is it? Yes or no? You're not allowed in here! It's dangerous! Speak up, what happened? Tell me! Right now!"

And then Henry had to tell the whole story — not to his father, and not to his mother, but to the mayor, the stern mayor with the scowl on his face.

Poor Henry! His legs shook and his hands trembled. But he had to tell.

He said, "I . . . I . . . I wanted to sail the wooden shoes on the water. I tied a string to them. Then I had two wooden shoes on a string. Two boats. They floated on the water and I held on to the string."

"Does your mother let you do that?"

"N-no. No. I did it without her knowing."

"And then?"

"Then I wanted to put two little sticks in them for

masts. But then the string
came loose. And one of the
wooden shoes drifted
away. And it was Lydia's."

"Yes, and then? Go on."

"That scared me so! And then I ran into your yard to
look for a stick to get the wooden shoe back and
then . . ."

Henry could not go on. He started to cry. But the
mayor said gruffly, "Don't cry! Go on with your
story. Come on."

"And then . . . and then you came. And you scared
me. So I hid in the stable. But then you came into
the stable too."

"So, you little spy! I didn't see you there. Where
were you?"

"I . . . I . . . I was hiding."

"Yes, but where were you hiding?"

"In the manger by the oats. You didn't see me."

The mayor couldn't help but laugh to himself. But
he did not want the boy to see him laugh so he bit
his lip.

"And the other wooden shoe. The one with the string. What happened to it?"

Henry wiped his tears away. Then he sobbed, "I put it in my pocket. But I lost it somehow. I don't have it anymore and now I can't find it."

"So, and now you've come back to the stable. But you know better. You're not allowed in here. Never! And now you've lost both your wooden shoes. Well, it's your own fault. Now get out of here — out of the stable, out of my yard! And watch out! If I ever catch you here again . . . !"

And then?

Oh, that poor little boy! He ran out of the stable, out of the yard, down the road. He sobbed with fear and grief. And he still did not have either one of the wooden shoes.

What would happen when Mother came home? When Father heard about it? He still had not told Father. Oh, that stern mayor!

But the little boy did not know that the mayor was watching him through the little window of the stable. Nor did he know that the mayor, that stern mayor, had a jolly smile on his face. Henry would never even have dreamed it!

He was so frightened and so very sad.

9. A Secret

Kuno, the big black horse, was happy. He was just as happy as his well-dressed master.

Together they rode out in the early morning air. All the birds sang.

Kuno pranced and neighed and threw back his big black head. White foam dripped from his mouth.

"What do you say? Shall we go fast this time — really fast, all out? I sure feel like it. Here we go!"

They galloped toward the windmill. The arms of the windmill were already turning.

The old miller's wife was sitting at the window looking out over the fields.

But then she saw the mayor coming — on horse back! She cried out, "Albert, Albert, here comes the mayor!"

The mayor tied his horse to a tree. "Wait here, Kuno."

Old Albert, the miller, came out to meet him. Together they stepped inside.

The mayor laughed merrily when he saw the two wooden shoes, the two twins, standing next to each other on the mantel. From one of them dangled a string. "There they are — both of them. Ha-ha-ha!" Then he said to the old miller and his wife, "Listen! I have come here to tell you something. It's my birthday on Saturday. Listen carefully to my idea."

The three sat down at the table — the mayor, the miller, and his old wife. They put their heads close together. The mayor whispered. He had a secret plan.

"Yes, yes. That's a good idea, Mr. Mayor. I'll take care of it," the old miller said and he scratched his head with delight.

"Yes, yes. Wonderful, Mr. Mayor," the old miller's wife said. "I'll be glad to help."

She could have danced with delight. But her old legs were too stiff. "Yes, yes! Won't Saturday be a great day?"

The mayor laughed.

"Ha-ha! There they stand — two wooden shoes, two little boats. Ha-ha-ha! The little rascal!"

Once again the mayor mounted his eager horse. Kuno pranced and neighed and snorted. He was having a

great time even though he knew nothing of the mayor's secret. He was happy because the sun shone and the birds sang — and because he was strong and ate lots of oats. He always enjoyed a good hard gallop too.

The old miller stood in the doorway. He was so delighted that he scratched his head with both his hands. His old wife sat at the window again. This time she was not looking out over the fields; she was watching the mayor. She watched him until he was out of sight. Softly she said to herself, "A good man. A fine man. And Saturday is his birthday. And that little rascal, that little monkey? That foolish little sailor? Ha-ha-ha!"

That day was a very busy day at the mill.
The old miller took a sack of floor out of the barn

— the finest, whitest flour he had. "They have to be good," he said.

He scratched his head.

The old woman washed her hands three times. They had to be clean. She was going to help too.

Then a horse and wagon rattled out to the mill from the village. The man in the wagon brought paper bags and little boxes and jars to the mill. What was going on?

Only the mayor, the old miller, and his wife knew.

It was a secret!

10. The Birthday Party

And then Saturday came . . .

The whole village rollicked with fun.

And the school children formed a parade.

The small ones marched in front with the teacher while the big ones followed behind with the principal. One of the biggest boys led the parade by beating a drum: boom-boom-boom! Three other boys played harmonicas. They were the band.

Henry marched right next to his teacher in the very first row.

He felt a bit flustered when he saw the mayor standing on the front steps of his beautiful house.

The mayor looked at the happy children and smiled. The happy children looked at him and smiled back. "Hurray!" they shouted. They were wishing him a happy birthday.

The mayor also looked at little Henry.

Henry's face turned very red. He did not shout "Hurray!" as loudly as the other children.

And then — then the parade marched out of the village, over the bridge, and down the road.

Where were they going?

To the windmill!

The children sang and shouted. And the band played on. Henry's face was back to normal again. Soon they were close to the windmill.

"Oh, do you smell that? Mm-m-m! Mm-m-m! Delicious!" The children's noses sniffed the air and their eyes lit up.

"Smells great! Mm-m-m! Mm-m-m!"

They were right next to the windmill.

What was it that smelled so good?

"Oh! Doughnuts! Doughnuts!"

The old miller beamed. His face shone with cooking oil and delight. He was still frying — making more and more of them. The golden oil had come from town in the jars. It sizzled in the huge pan that stood out in the yard. The doughnuts were white when they went in, but they came out a beautiful golden brown. The dough was made of the finest, whitest flour the miller had. And with her clean hands the old miller's wife had mixed in raisins and currants and tiny bits of apple. Mm-m-m! Mm-m-m! Delicious!

The old woman sat at the open window. This time she did not look out over the fields. Not at all. She looked at all the happy children. She smiled and waved at them. "Fine children. Wonderful children." She also shone — not with cooking oil, but with joy. The children sat down in the grass in a big circle.

Then the policeman stepped into the middle of the circle. He scowled, but that did not mean he was angry.

And then the party began — the mayor's birthday party with lots and lots of doughnuts.

Mm-m-m! Mm-m-m! Delicious!

Henry sat next to his teacher.

The miller kept on frying and the policeman passed the doughnuts out on a huge platter. The doughnuts were covered with white powdered sugar. They smelled good — and tasted even better! The doughnuts kept coming — more and more of them. Platter after platter.

Little Henry also enjoyed the doughnuts. But he could not help thinking about that wooden shoe, the one that the miller had kept. Where was that wooden shoe? Was it inside the windmill somewhere? Or was it in the little house next to the windmill, where the miller's wife was sitting by the open window? Or perhaps in the barn? He did not know. And now Lydia had no wooden shoes.

When Mother had come back from her trip he had been punished. For two days he had not been allowed to play outdoors. And the policeman had come over to talk to Mother. Henry had been terrified for the policeman worked closely with the mayor. Henry did not know what the policeman had told Mother.

It was strange though. The policeman had laughed. And then Mother had laughed too. Mother had said, "That's fine, Officer. That's fine. Do whatever you want with him."

That sure was strange. Henry did not understand it. And now, at the mayor's birthday party, he kept one worried eye on the policeman.

But the doughnuts were so good that soon he forgot all about the policeman again — and he even forgot about the wooden shoes.

"Look!" cried the boys. "Look!"

"Hurray! Hurray!"

The mayor came riding that big black horse of his. He waved his hat.

11. In the Bag

Kuno swished his tail from side to side. He chased the flies away. But he would have liked to chase the children away too. "Whew! What a racket! Let's go. Let's just gallop off."

But Kuno was tied to a tree.

So he tried to snatch a tasty mouthful of grass.

The mayor walked into the circle and all the children cheered.

"Hurray! Hurray!" That meant, "The party's great! Just wonderful!"

The mayor sat down on an overturned pail to eat one of the doughnuts.

Then he stood up. "Officer," he said. "It's time for the bags."

What did that mean?

The policeman passed out paper bags to the children. And the teachers were given bags too. But why?

Oh, but then the children understood. They would each get a few doughnuts to take home with them. Wonderful!

Then the policeman walked into the house standing next to the windmill.

But why? No one knew.

But soon they had forgotten all about the policeman. They were thinking about the delicious doughnuts they would get in their bags.

The little boy sitting next to his teacher was to be first. That was Henry.

All the children watched. His teacher led him to the open window where the miller's friendly wife sat. Beside her was a table piled high with doughnuts — a huge mountain of doughnuts. She was going to put a few doughnuts into each child's bag. She beamed with delight. She had forgotten all about her stiff legs.

There stood Henry by the open window. His eyes sparkled. He held up the open bag with both his hands.

But — poor Henry! The mayor came to the window too! The mayor said, "You little rascal! I know you." Henry was frightened and turned beet red.

"So, you want to take something home with you too, do you?" asked the mayor.

"Yes, sir," Henry said softly.

"Something for your little sister?" asked the mayor. "Do you love your little sister?"

"Yes, sir," Henry nodded. But he felt ashamed. He hung his head. The mayor knew everything about

Lydia's wooden shoes. "Hold your bag open, wide open — with both hands."

Henry stood right by the window, his head down, his bag wide open. And then?

Plop!

Something fell from above. It fell right down past the little boy's nose — something white and round and hard. It plopped right into Henry's bag.

It scared Henry! The bag shook in his hands. He was about to look up when . . .

Plop!

Something else fell from above. It fell right down past the little boy's nose — something white and round and hard. It landed in his bag right on top of the other one.

Poor startled Henry! The bag slipped out of his hands and fell down at his feet, with those two white, round, hard things inside. The bag flopped shut.

Henry still could not see what was inside. He looked straight up but he could not see anything.

All the other children, the teachers, the mayor, the miller, his friendly wife at the window — they were all laughing. They howled and roared with laughter at Henry, poor startled little Henry. He looked so frightened and so funny!

"Ha-ha-ha, Henry. They're good, Henry. Why don't you take a bite? Ha-ha-ha!"

They had all seen something that Henry had not seen. They had seen a little window open above the window where the miller's wife sat. The policeman had peeked out. Quickly he had dropped two white, hard, round things.

Plop! Right in Henry's bag. Quickly he had slipped back inside and closed the window again.

And those things? Why . . . they were . . . they were . . .

Funny, frightened Henry! He still did not know.

The mayor laughed. "Why don't you look and see what you've got in your bag, you little rascal?" Henry picked up his bag. He looked.

What? Could it be? The wooden shoes! Lydia's two wooden shoes — both of them!

The smiling children looked on with big eyes.

The miller's wife said, "Just put those wooden shoes down in the grass for now. And bring your bag over here."

Then Henry got some doughnuts after all, not round, white, hard ones, but real doughnuts — soft and brown and delicious.

Henry got four doughnuts to take home, one for each member of the family.

Then the others got their turns to come to the window, to the big mountain of doughnuts.

Then, with everyone carrying a brown bag, the parade headed back to the village, the band leading the way.

At the head of the parade, next to his teacher, walked Henry. His eyes sparkled and his cheeks glowed. He carried the bag of doughnuts in front of him. He carried the wooden shoes under his arms — one under each arm. One of the wooden shoes had a string dangling from it.

And so — so the wooden shoes came home after all — they came home to Lydia.

12. Evening

That evening the old miller and his wife sat at their table. They were tired from all the day's doings because they were getting old. But they still chuckled.

"That mayor — what a joker! He planned it all and he paid for it all," said the old woman. "And what a

beautiful secret it was! First the doughnuts and then the wooden shoes in Henry's bag. Ha-ha-ha!"

"And the policeman dropped them just right," said the old miller.

"And those children!" said the miller's wife. "Good children. Wonderful children. But I still have not seen the little girl whose wooden shoes those were. That's too bad."

"Yes, that is too bad," said the miller, "because it was her wooden shoe that floated on the water . . ."

That evening Father smoked his pipe in front of the house. He had eaten his doughnut. The policeman walked by. He stopped and said, "That was some party!"

Father answered, "Yes, that was some party! We knew all about it because you told Henry's mother the whole plan. But we did not tell him. No, sir! Henry did not know a thing about it — the little rascal!"

The policeman laughed, "We certainly pulled one over on him, didn't we? Wooden shoes in his bag! Ha-ha-ha! It worked out just right. The mayor thought of everything."

"Yes," said Father. "He sure is a fine mayor. Sometimes he looks stern but he has a heart of gold."

Mother came outside to join in the talk and the laughter. "What a fine joke it was!" she said. "And tomorrow I'm going over to the windmill myself. I want to thank those two dear old people for what they did. And I'll take Lydia along, wearing her wooden shoes. After all, it was her wooden shoe that floated on the water . . . "

That evening each father and mother in the village had a delicious doughnut to eat. The children had brought them home in their paper bags.

Kuno, the big, black horse, did not like doughnuts. He rather had oats. After he went to sleep, his little friend the mouse came back into the stable to eat his fill of oats too.

But his pretty little crib to sleep in, the sturdy wooden crib with a roof on it, was gone.

He did not know where it had gone. So he curled up in a dark corner of the manger. That was also a good place to sleep.

That evening a little boy knelt down by his bed.

His hands were folded and his eyes were closed. And he was very happy!

He said his usual bedtime prayer. Then he whispered, "Dear Lord, I'm so happy tonight! It was my fault about the wooden shoes. And now we have them back. I'm so happy!"

Then he crawled into bed. His window stood open. He could hear his father and his mother and the policeman talk.

He could not make out what they were saying. But he could tell they were laughing. They were happy too.

They were not angry at him anymore.

And he was not afraid of the mayor anymore.

All the fear was gone from his heart.

He snuggled down deep under his blankets.

Would he sail again? Would he sail Lydia's wooden shoes again? No, never again!

Before long he was asleep.

Then, once more, but only for a moment, he saw the wooden shoe float on the water . . .

But this time it was only a dream.

Titles in this series: